Thomas H. Harding

Toothache and other Affections of the Teeth

SALZWASSER
VERLAG

Thomas H. Harding

Toothache and other Affections of the Teeth

Reprint of the original, first published in 1859.

1st Edition 2022 | ISBN: 978-3-37513-392-4

Verlag (Publisher): Salzwasser Verlag GmbH, Zeilweg 44, 60439 Frankfurt, Deutschland
Vertretungsberechtigt (Authorized to represent): E. Roepke, Zeilweg 44, 60439 Frankfurt, Deutschland
Druck (Print): Books on Demand GmbH, In de Tarpen 42, 22848 Norderstedt, Deutschland

TOOTHACHE

AND OTHER AFFECTIONS OF THE

TEETH

RELIEVED BY THE

ELECTRIC CAUTERY.

BY

THOMAS H. HARDING,

SURGEON DENTIST.

SECOND EDITION.

LONDON:

WALTON AND MABERLY,

UPPER GOWER STREET, & IVY LANE, PATERNOSTER ROW.

1859.

Price One Shilling.

OPINIONS OF THE PRESS.

"This work fully shows the value of the electric cautery in dentistry."—THE LANCET.

"The importance of the subject, coupled with the lucid manner in which it is handled, renders the essay worthy of being strongly recommended to the profession in the convenient separate form in which it is now published."—QUARTERLY JOURNAL OF DENTAL SCIENCE.

"It is said that by this process toothache is often cured, and the diseased tooth may remain serviceable for many years."—MED. TIMES AND GAZETTE.

"The advantages of the electric cautery over the actual cautery consist in the facility with which the amount of heat may be regulated, and in the light given off by the wire, which enables the operator to apply the cautery to the sensitive pulp only, without carbonizing the cavity of the tooth."—PHARMACEUTICAL JOURNAL.

"The perusal of the interesting little *brochure* by Mr. HARDING will impress the reader favorably with its merits. * * * * It commends itself as affording a quick and simple means, which will compare favorably with other expedients more commonly resorted to for relief from a very sore and much prevailing malady."—MONTREAL MEDICAL CHRONICLE.

"Toothache is really such a formidable malady, that we are glad to inform our readers of any quick and effectual means of cure."—MEDICAL CIRCULAR.

ADVERTISEMENT.

The flattering reception which the first edition of this little volume has met with, as evidenced in its rapid sale ; and the favourable manner in which it has been noticed by the Medical and Dental Journals, in this country and in America, has convinced me that my humble efforts in the cause of Dental Science have been appreciated.

With some additions and alterations in the present edition, I have only to add that increased experience has more fully confirmed all that is stated throughout its pages.

T. H. H.

19, PARK SQUARE EAST,
REGENT'S PARK,
September, 1858.

ADVERTISEMENT TO THE FIRST EDITION.

The greater part of the following pages appeared in the Lancet; a desire having been expressed to see the matter in a separate form, has induced me to publish this little volnme, which is submitted to my brethren of the Dental Profession.

T. H. H.

TABLE OF CONTENTS.

THE

ELECTRIC CAUTERY

AND

ITS APPLICATION TO DENTAL SURGERY.

IT will be as well, at the commencement of
the present essay, just to glance at the
HISTORY of the introduction of the Electric
cautery, and its general application in surgical
practice.   Crusell, of St. Petersburgh, was the
first to employ it for surgical operations, and
although his researches generally on its use
were not published before the year 1846, yet
his operations bear date anterior to those of
any other surgeon.

In 1844, M. Louyet, of Brussels, recommended the operation for destroying the dental nerve; and in 1845, Heider, of Vienna, at the instigation of Steinheil, of Munich, cauterized the dental nerves with the galvanic cautery. In 1850, Mr. Marshall was the first to employ it in practical surgery in this country, but his researches were not published before 1851, when he brought the subject before the Royal Medical and Chirurgical Society in April of that year. In the same year I published a short paper on its use in dental surgery, being the first to adopt it in that special branch of surgery in this coun·try; and in the same journal ("The Lancet") a paper also appeared from Mr. Waite, recom·mending its use in dentistry.

Since 1851, it has been generally employed by others in England, France, and Germany.

Being deeply impressed with the great value of this powerful agent in many of the most delicate operations which come under the hand of the general surgeon, from reading the papers communicated to the Medico-Chirurgical Society by my friend, Mr. Marshall, in which the results showed most satisfactorily the great value of this new agent; it struck me that its introduction into the practice of dental surgery would prove of inestimable value and of the greatest possible assistance, in effectually destroying the sensitive pulp of a decayed tooth, in a more certain, rapid, and safe manner than any of the numerous methods with which dentists are already familiar. I therefore conceived the idea, that a platinum wire, heated in the manner as recommended by Mr. Marshall, might be made available for the instantaneous destruction of an exposed tooth-pulp. I accordingly communicated my idea to Mr. Marshall, who fully concurred with me as to its importance. It had already suggested itself to his fertile mind, and had been mentioned by him as one of the obvious applications of his method of operating with the electric heat. His experience in this matter, moreover, enabled him to suggest for the purpose a very simple and suitable apparatus, which shall shortly be described.

In the first volume of "The Lancet" for 1851, there appeared a short communication from me on the destruction of the dental pulp by the heat of electricity, wherein I confidently stated that it might be regarded as a great advantage by all engaged in the practice of dental surgery. I had employed it for some months previous to the appearance of that paper, and fairly and justly claim to have been the first to use it in dental surgery in this country. In the same number of that journal was described an instrument for applying heat in dental operations, by Mr. Waite; but I had used it before the time mentioned by Mr. Waite, and moreover was not acquainted with his invention.

Now, other methods have been employed for applying heat to destroy the nerve of an aching tooth. The qld village doctress has long been famous for curing toothache by the thrust of a hot needle or pin into the tooth, and dentists have occasionally used a heated wire. The actual cautery has long been a practice in vogue for the purpose of destroying the sensibility of the tooth-pulp from caries, and has been generally performed by heating a long piece of steel, small at one end, but terminating in a bulbous head about the size of a small pea, which is in-inserted into a handle. From the bulbous extremity projects a piece of platinum wire, smaller or larger according to circumstances: the bulbous end being heated in an ordinary lamp until a red or white heat is obtained, communicates the heat to the platinum wire, which is then immediately used for the purposes required. Another method of applying hot wires to the teeth is by means of platinum sponge and hydrogen gas, known as Œropile; but I have had no experience of the use of this.

In regard to the use of the actual cautery, let us see what Mr. Snell says of it in his book on the teeth : he writes, "Even now, it (the destruction by the actual cautery) is frequently performed in an improper manner, which will account for the want of success which often attends it when attempted by ignorant men. As the operation is very generally performed, it would be more properly styled carbonizing the cavity of the tooth generally, then simply cauterizing the membrane." It must be obvious to everyone that the great cause of failure, such as is here described, depends upon the difficulty experienced in obtaining a sufficient and permanent amount of heat; for it is well known that wire alone, which is the only substance sufficiently minute to be applied within the interior of a tooth, can retain the heat but for a very limited time. It is therefore necessary, in the hands of some dental surgeons, who are not satisfied with its effects, to apply it to the tooth certainly more than once, perhaps several times in succession. This must prove of serious injury to the teeth, as it will carbonize a large surface of the tooth generally, instead of cauterizing or destroying the tooth-pulp solely. Now all this is completely removed by the use of the electric cautery, which can never be surpassed for convenience and ready mode of application, besides possessing a steady, uniform, and constant degree of heat, which can be retained at pleasure until the proper effects are obtained, and then as magically discontinued by destroying the connexion between the positive and negative wires. It has the advantage also, over every other known method of cauterizing, that it can be introduced into the patient's mouth, and actually placed within the cavity of the tooth, before it is made to become incandescent,—an advantage that cannot be over-estimated by those conscientious dental surgeons who are so frequently called upon to destroy a tooth-pulp.

THE NATURE OF THE APPARATUS.

The nature of the apparatus which I am in the habit of using may be thus described. I shall first speak of the battery, and then of the cauterizer :—

The BATTERY is a compound one of Smee's, and consists of six pairs of plates of zinc and platinized silver, contained in six cells, which are set in action by one fluid—viz., dilute sulphuric acid. The battery may of course vary according to the choice and taste of the operator, but it is desirable to render it as elegant and as simple as possible. When I first employed the electric cautery, I used a battery of two pairs of plates in a single cell. I now prefer the larger battery of six cells, because a large battery with weak acid will last longer than a small one with strong acid; besides this, the action of the battery is more uniform, and lasts much longer. A Smee's battery is the most convenient in application: it is always clean, ready when wanted, and has the advantage moreover of cheapness. Grove's and Maynooth's batteries are not fitted for the purpose required, as they are troublesome, and often give out fumes of nitrous acid, which are decidedly objectionable.

The CAUTERIZER is thus constituted:—The terminal six inches of the poles, which are of copper wire plated, are supported on an ebony or ivory handle, upon the side of which, one of the poles is interrupted at a particular point. The extremities of the poles are connected by a piece of platinum wire, a hundredth part of an inch thick, and three-quarters of an inch long, which is bent into a loop. The sides of the loop are then brought parallel and nearly close to each other, without touching ; and it is thus introduced into the pulp cavity of the tooth to be operated on. By a slight pressure on one side of the handle, the interrupted pole is temporarily joined, and the platinum wire immediately becomes brilliantly heated, as it lies in contact with the tooth-pulp. Sometimes, however, I have found it desirable in the first place, to complete the galvanic current, and thus heat the platinum wire before bringing it to bear upon the exposed pulp. The flexibility of the loop of wire enables the operator to bend it in any direction previously to use. In this way I have succeeded in rapidly destroying the pulps of decayed and condemned teeth, and have proceeded, sometimes after a few minutes, to the operation of filling them with gold, or with other suitable stoppings, as Ash's metallic paste. I use several cauterizers with extremely thin wires, made expressly for myself by Ash and Sons, of Broad-street, Golden-square.*

OF THE OPERATION IN GENERAL.

The affected tooth having been carefully examined, its cavity is to be well-dried out and cleaned : a soft napkin is then introduced to protect the mouth from the possibility of contact with the instrument, the platinum point of which, being passed into the cavity of the tooth, is then heated, and from its brilliancy, gives a clear and distinct light, and the tooth-pulp is gently touched with the heated wire, and the whole, or

---

* A very perfect electric cautery apparatus, made on an improved principle, under the Author's superintendance, has been prepared by Messrs. Ash and Sons, of Broad-street, Golden-square, which not only fully answers the purpose for which it is recommended by the Author, but is sold at a more moderate price than any hitherto manufactured.

particular portion of it required, is destroyed. If the operator prefer it, he may have the wire heated before introduction into the mouth; but my own practice is generally to apply the wire before doing this, and then permitting incandescence to take place in the mouth, which gives a light which is not seen by the patient, and so well illuminates the interior of the tooth, as to permit the tooth-pulp or diseased membrane to be seen very distinctly and clearly.

There is some caution to be observed in the use of this agent, which it will be as well to mention, and that is, to avoid burning or otherwise injuring the solid part of the tooth. Particular attention and care should be paid to this point. This will not happen unless the application is prolonged, which will very rarely indeed be required, if special care be observed to have the wire at a white heat. This is the more necessary to produce speedy destruction of the part to be touched, which is effected almost instantaneously. In one instance under my care, that of a lady for whom I nipped off the crown of an incisor tooth, for the purpose of fixing some artificial teeth, and so exposed the pulp of that tooth, I applied the electric cautery at barely a red heat, owing to feebleness of the acid; the consequence of this was, that the dental pulp became attached to the end of the wire, and was actually drawn out entirely. This has been preserved. It gave some slight pain for the moment, but nothing in comparison to the pointed steel or silver wire used by most dentists. This perhaps unimportant accident, I think, would not have occurred had the cautery been at a white heat, as it would then have completely carbonized or destroyed the part with which it came into contact.

The EFFECT of the operation is the rapid destruction of the pulps of the decayed and condemned teeth; not the whole of the pulp for that is not always necessary, but that portion of

C

it especially which is exposed. If this is done with a light, steady hand, no subsequent inflammation is produced upon the substance of the tooth, or in the cavity. If there should be any marked sensitiveness in the tooth, independent of the pulp, the slightest application of the cautery to it will prove effectual in completely removing it. In the large number of cases in which I have employed the electric cautery I have never known any bad effects produced on the tooth : and this I attribute to the care with which it has been applied. I am, however, quite prepared to believe that a want of attention in this respect would not only prove injurious to the tooth, but even in many instances cause its destruction. It would be only under such circumstances that the operation could be attended with or followed by severe pain.

In whatever condition the tooth-pulp may be, the operation is associated with a little pain. But as the time of its application is not unfre-

quently just a second or so, in the large majority
of instances in which I have employed it there
has been no pain whatever felt.   There may be
a sort of twinge, which is but momentary; and
whatever pain may follow is not to be compared
to that arising from the process of extracting
a tooth, which, as is well known, is always
attended by a very considerable amount of
pain.   Some of my patients have felt so little
when it has been applied, that they have asked
me to apply it a second time to make all certain that the dental pulp has been effectually
destroyed.

The SUBSEQUENT FILLING OF THE TOOTH is a
matter which demands attention after the pulp
is destroyed. If the cavity is examined very
minutely, a small black speck or spot can be
seen after the cautery has been used.   This is
due to the carbonization of the pulp, and is a
guide to some extent in the after process of removal of the carious portion of the tooth, which

should always be effected after the sensibility has been destroyed by the electric cautery. This is to be accomplished with care in the usual manner, taking the precaution to leave none of the tooth in that condition remaining : every particle of it should be removed. For a few days afterwards, sometimes only one, but generally two, the cavity is allowed to remain filled with a combination of morphine and mastich, and then the tooth is stopped. Sometimes, again, I request my patients to allow a few days to elapse before I stop their teeth, the cavities being in the meantime filled with a solution of mastich and camphor. But I occasionally accomplish what I believe no other dentist has done, and that is, to plug, or stop the cavity at the same sitting during which the nerve has been destroyed. This, however, depends upon the complete absence of pain after the use of the cautery. I have already stated there is always a little pain ; but sometimes this at once disappears, and I then do not hesitate to stop the tooth permanently. I also stop the tooth immediately if there has been a little bleeding from the cavity previous to cauterization. It might be supposed this procedure of stopping the teeth, immediately after the destruction of the pulp, would be always followed by dull, aching pain; but I am happy to say that not the slightest indication has, in the great majority of instances, ensued, in rather an extensive use of this powerful agent.

As a rule, however, the tooth should not be stopped on the same day that the electric cautery has been applied, unless in the exceptional cases just mentioned—the removal of the carious portion not being followed by sensibility. Experience and practice teach us to know the proper cases which can be plugged immediately.

By waiting a day or two, I have found by experience also, that any sensibility remaining after the destruction of the dental pulp, and the removal of the carious parts of the affected tooth, is sure to disappear, assisted by the solution of morphine and mastich, or mastich and camphor, which occupies the cavity. By this time the cavity will bear the pressure of an instrument within it, and an examination will show that the destroyed pulp has receded considerably inwards. This is apparent by noticing the black discoloration from the previous carbonization of the affected part, and, as it is deeply situated, it is either out of the way of being pressed upon by the stopping of the tooth, or becomes a matter of the smallest possible importance, so far as my experience enables me to judge in this respect. I must, however, warn others not to mistake the black speck here referred to for actual caries.

Under the various circumstances which have been mentioned, the RESULTS of the operation are completely successful, and the teeth are serviceable for years. If, however, a tooth should remain tender after the use of the cautery, it is always better to wait for its complete insensibility before proceeding to stopping. I cannot call to mind any single instance in which the pain was at all persistent after its use; but it will be sure to become so, if the tooth is one not fairly suitable for preservation, from being either loose, or diseased at the termination of a fang, such as a small fungous growth, or other similar cause. In such cases, as I will shortly show, the destruction of the tooth-pulp, accomplished no matter by what method, will prove unavailing and unsatisfactory, ultimate extraction in such instances proving the only resource. Should there be associated inflammation of the gums with a carious tooth, in which the pulp has been destroyed in the manner which has been recommended, then the usual means for combating it must be resorted to,—such as a leech or two to the gum, and repeated fomentations with warm water alone, as I am in the habit of recommending, or with warm milk and water, or a poultice. For the pain in the tooth itself, morphine and mastich will be found quite sufficient.

Some patients express the receipt of immediate relief after the use of the cautery ; others, again, not for an hour or two, but eventually are quite relieved : the pain, however, I repeat, is extremely slight.

In the large number of cases in which I have used the electric cautery to destroy the sensitive tooth-pulp, I have not known an ACCIDENT, in the true sense of the word, to happen, unless I should except the case in which the dental pulp was suddenly drawn out attached to the platinum wire, which I have preserved for illustration, and depending upon, as has been said, the wire being at a red instead of a white heat. Such a circumstance might occur again in the hands of others. To avoid injury or accidents to the teeth or gums, it is necessary to keep the hand quiet, firm, and steady. The heated wires, if suddenly dislodged, would assuredly burn the cheek or gums, the tongue or palate, especially if steadiness was not particularly observed on the part of the patient. It may be observed, however, that so rapidly can the disconnexion of the wires be accomplished by removal of the finger from the handle of the instrument, that an accident can really very seldom occur from the heated wire.

Having thus considered the history of the use of the electric cautery in general surgery, its application to dentistry, the nature of the apparatus employed, and the general features of the operation, together with its effects and results, I shall in the next place make a few observations upon the cases which are suitable, and upon those which are unfitted for its use; and will then draw a comparison between the use of the cautery and other methods of destroying the pulp.

OF THE OPERATION IN PARTICULAR.

The great object of this operation, which I am endeavouring so strongly to recommend in the present volume, is to destroy the irritable ulcer in the membrane of the tooth which permits the nerve to be exposed, and which is often associated with the presence and even protrusion of minute granulations, not dissimilar to what the surgeon meets with as protruding from an ulcer situated over a carious or necrosed bone in some other part of the body. This condition is accompanied with a certain amount of inflammation and tumefaction. The cautery, as I have said before, completely destroys the affected parts, and there is no time left to produce a new surface: nor do I think that could be accomplished after the destruction of the pulp ; nor, again, is it a necessary measure, as no particular good could be derived from it, were it to be permitted to occur.

The cavity is at once plugged and the admission of air to the tooth prevented, and the sensitiveness and carious condition are permanently removed.

Now of the PROPER CASES in which the electric cautery may be used, the most important and common is that known as severe ordinary toothache,—especially that form of tooth affection arising from a cavity with exposure of the tooth-pulp. In cases also of cavities requiring filling, in which too great a sensitiveness is present, thus preventing the satisfactory removal of the carious portions of the tooth, it is equally valuable. It is useful also in cases where the gums have receded, with exposure of a part of the neck of a tooth, which is extremely sensitive and oftentimes very painful to the touch. In these it is necessary merely to touch the exposed necks, to remove the sensitiveness. It is not less serviceable in its application to tender, sensitive, and bleeding gums, producing a new and healthy action, which permits them to become firmly

attached again to the necks of the previously-
exposed teeth. Sometimes it is merely necessary
to hold the heated wire near a sensitive neck,
without actual contact, to remove the tenderness. I have destroyed, with the greatest ease
and rapidity, the pulps of incisor teeth which
have been cut off for the purpose of being
pivoted. Every dentist is aware of the sensitiveness which sometimes exists in a pivoted
incisor tooth, depending upon the vitality of the
stump; this is completely obviated by the use
of the cautery. I have employed it also in
numberless instances in which unusual sensitiveness exists to both warm and cold substances,
depending upon a variety of causes: such as
exposure of the necks; or arising from chipping
and fracture of the tooth from brittleness or
some other cause; or, again, where the tooth
has been filed, cut, or accidently broken. A
very striking instance of this kind—that is, un-
usually great suffering from taking either warm

or cold liquids into the mouth—came under
my care, in which permanent and complete
relief was afforded from the electric cautery.
If a tooth is snapped off at the neck, and
the pulp-cavity becomes exposed and painful,
it can be destroyed, and an artificial tooth may
be fastened to the stump, in the same manner
as when the tooth is intentionally removed
for this purpose. Sometimes, also, bleeding
will occur from the rupture of some minute
capillary vessels during the removal of caries
from a cavity which may have become morbidly
vascular, without the presence of actual pain or
even sensitiveness. It is equally serviceable here
as in other forms of disease, and stops the hæ-
morrhage, which is inconvenient and troublesome, from its interference with the progress of
stopping the tooth. I have also applied it in
sensitiveness arising from the wearing away or
grooving of a tooth, from the constant pressure
of the spring clasp of a plate, which has caused

the destruction of the dentine ; mechanical friction, in fact, producing this condition.

As a general rule, the electric cautery may be used with decided advantage in almost every case of diseased tooth, with very few exceptions. But the commonest affection CONSTANTLY requiring its use, I again repeat, is ordinary TOOTHACHE, not unfrequently most agonizing in its character, and depending upon the presence of a cavity from caries, which has laid bare the delicate nervous pulp contained in it, which, so long as it is likely to come into contact with the liquids and solids of the mouth, will continue in this condition. Destruction of the pulp and subsequent stopping prove the remedy : the nerve is destroyed, the pain disappears, and the tooth remains for years, and answers as well as if it had been filled without exposure and destruction of the pulp.

The electric cautery therefore saves many a tooth which, without its aid, would be otherwise

totally lost. It is preserved for years, and
perhaps it is not saying too much, that if ordinary care and precaution are used, it will most
probably last the life-time of the individual.
This, perhaps, may seem to be problematical, as
many dentists would declare that, if the nerve
is destroyed, the tooth is dead : it is a foreign
body, will last but a few years, ultimately de-
cay, and require extraction. The cautery certainly destroys either a portion or the whole of
the dental or nervous pulp ; I will say, for
argument's sake, that it does completely and
effectually destroy the nerve of the tooth. The
tooth, however, receives nourishment from the
periostium covering its fang, as well as from that
lining its socket, and it would seem that there
may even be minute nervous twigs accompany-
ing the equally minute capillary bloodvessels
which afford life and sustenance to the plugged
tooth. It cannot therefore be looked upon as
a foreign body, as it possesses and retains its

vitality, which is derived through its fang, or, in
other words, from without, and is thus capable,
from the reasons mentioned, of lasting with
proper care, the patient's lifetime. Mr. Nasmyth
has beautifully shown in his work on the Teeth,
that a tooth is supplied with a large number of
minute nervous twigs and bloodvessels.

I must also speak of another form of affection
which has been relieved by it, namely, neuralgia
of the face—a form of tic douloureux, supposed
to depend upon some other cause than a carious
tooth. On examining the mouth, however, I
have detected an affected tooth, on destroying
the pulp of which with the cautery, and subse-
quently stopping it, a permanent cure has been
effected.

It may be recommended as admirably suited
to destroy fungous growths springing from the
internal pulp, which often bleed very profusely
on the slightest touch.

It will thus be seen that the application of

the electric cautery is wide and extensive, in the number and variety of the cases of tooth disease.

The following, however, ARE UNFIT FOR IT, as it would not only produce no good, but harm might result from its use :—

When a tooth is loose, with its external aspect sound, but the pain depending upon the presence of a fungous growth or small abscess developed at the end of one or more of the fangs. In such a case extraction only will afford relief.

It will prove of no avail, in an attack of inflammation of the central pulp, which may sometimes affect a tooth that is otherwise apparently sound This may be known by the severe, heavy, throbbing pain which it occasions, running up to the head, accompanied with considerable tenderness of the tooth and the gum around it. This condition may go on to suppuration of the pulp, or to abscess of the alveolus, and consequent death of the tooth. Leeches are here useful conjoined with some slight constitutional treatment.

E

And, lastly, when we find a black, unsightly tooth lying loose in its socket, with pain depending upon the irritation produced by its presence, the cautery will be ineffectual, as the tooth is in a true state of necrosis, is quite dead, and has truly become a foreign body; it must therefore be removed. This condition I have not unfrequently seen to depend upon the use or abuse of mercury.

If a COMPARISON be now instituted between the electric cautery, as I am in the habit of employing it for destroying the tooth-pulp, and the numerous other means recommended to effect the same purpose, it will be seen that the balance of my confirmed judgment is entirely in favour of the former. Thus the great advantage of the cautery is, that the desired effect is produced in less time than a minute; whilst it takes days, and even months, to accomplish destruction of the pulp by the various substances habitually in use: amongst these may

be mentioned arsenic, used either alone or
in combination with other substances, as, for
instance, a mixture of equal parts of arsenic,
morphine, and creosote ; chloride of zinc, in the
solid form, or a combination of it and chloroform; cobalt, chloroform, creosote, gun-cotton,
tannin, and tannate of lead. Nitrate of silver is
used ; or nitric acid on a gold wire. Many other
substances are employed. The nausea produced
by the use of chloride of zinc, or nitrate of silver,
is particularly disagreeable. I have, however,
the strongest objection to the use of arsenic, more
so than to any other substance ; and it is not
without much thought on the subject, that I
have come to the conclusion that it ought not to
be employed in dental surgery. I have known
instances in which this agent has been used, and
the most acute and severe pain—in fact, absolute
torture—has followed for several days, before
stopping the cavity could be accomplished. Besides the pain, there is also the danger arising

from its absorption. A few months ago a case of fatal poisoning appeared in the journals, which depended upon its absorption after employment in a dental operation. Added to the time required to destroy a tooth-pulp by these various substances, there is also the mischief caused by their local application to the teeth themselves, which should not be lost sight of in the consideration of this question.

CONCLUSIONS.—I have now been in the habit of employing the electric cautery for upwards of eight years, and during that time have used it in more than six thousand instances, with an amount of success that has surpassed my most sanguine expectations, and without the occurence of a single accident worthy of mention. I may truly say, that there are very few cases of toothache which cannot be relieved by it, when the membrane or tooth-pulp can be got at to destroy it. These very few cases are the exceptional in-

stances which have already been referred to   It
has been held by writers on diseases of the teeth,
that the impossibility of instantaneously effecting
the absolute destruction of the tooth-pulp in such
as are situated at the back of the mouth, which
possess several diverging roots, is a sufficient
ground for rejecting the means which were employed for that purpose—namely, the heating of
a wire, in the form of the actual cautery, which
cannot at any time be maintained at a white
heat.   It was in consequence of this very great
difficulty that the actual cautery has fallen into
disuse.   Now the advantage which the electric
cautery has over every other conceivable method
is, that the white heat produced, and which
cannot be obtained in any other manner, effects
the purpose desired suddenly and with com-
pleteness.   Besides this, it can be applied with
perfect ease and freedom to teeth situated in any
part of the mouth without the risk or danger of
burning it—a risk almost impossible to avoid,

with the greatest care, when the actual cautery or heated iron was employed.

It might be supposed, again, that some imaginary terror is likely to be excited in the patient's mind, at the idea of the electric cautery, in the shape of an incandescent body being used for any purpose in the mouth. I can truly say, that in the large amount of experience of its use which has fallen to my lot, that there is not the slightest ground for such a supposition. If this be an objection to its employment, then it falls to the ground, for I can call to mind no instance wherein this fear was manifested. Sometimes, as has been before mentioned, the wire is introduced already heated into the mouth, when being applied to the tooth.

At one time much dread of the actual cautery arose, from the burning of the mouth by the heated handle of the instrument, which was unavoidably employed to keep the wire hot, and this occasioned, we believe, its comparative re-

jection in this country. With the electric cautery such accidents are avoided. I may say, they
scarcely ever occur in the hands of any ordi-
narily skilful man; for, owing to the extreme fine-
ness of the wire employed, the local heat, though
intense, is very limited in its action, and with
due care the tooth substance need not suffer any
appreciable injury. For the same reason, with
the additional and more powerful one, of suddenly breaking the connection between the poles
of the battery, no injury can happen to the
mouth or gums.

Such, then, are the uses and advantages of
this valuable agent in dental practice, and so
well known is it becoming to a large number of
the public, that a considerable proportion of my
patients come recommended to me by medical
men and others, for the express purpose of cauterization by it.

In March, 1857, a lady, to two of whose teeth
I applied it instead of extracting them, writes to

me, "Neither of my teeth has given me the least uneasiness. I am sure I have much to thank your for. Now, one need not fear the approach of toothache ; we are so much more favoured than those who lived a hundred years ago." These two teeth were, I may observe cauterized and stopped at the same sitting.

I can now with still greater confidence, and much larger experience, lay this most valuable and efficient remedy before the notice of my professional brethren than I did in 1851. Very many years' constant trial have only further convinced me, that for ingenuity, simplicity of contrivance and application, nothing that has hitherto been invented can surpass it. And I again confidently leave it in their hands, gladly availing myself of my connection with the College of Dentists, as one of its members, as a med·ium of doing so.